# WELCOME TO PASSPORT TO READING

**A beginning reader's ticket to a brand-new world!**

Every book in this program is designed to build read-along and read-alone skills, level by level, through engaging and enriching stories. As the reader turns each page, he or she will become more confident with new vocabulary, sight words, and comprehension.

These PASSPORT TO READING levels will help you choose the perfect book for every reader.

**READING TOGETHER**
Read short words in simple sentence structures together to begin a reader's journey.

**READING OUT LOUD**
Encourage developing readers to sound out words in more complex stories with simple vocabulary.

**READING INDEPENDENTLY**
Newly independent readers gain confidence reading more complex sentences with higher word counts.

**READY TO READ MORE**
Readers prepare for chapter books with fewer illustrations and longer paragraphs.

This book features sight words from the educator-supported Dolch Sight Word List. Readers will become more familiar with these commonly used vocabulary words, increasing reading speed and fluency.

For more information, please visit www.passporttoreadingbooks.com, where each reader can add stamps to a personalized passport while traveling through story after story!



*Enjoy the journey!*

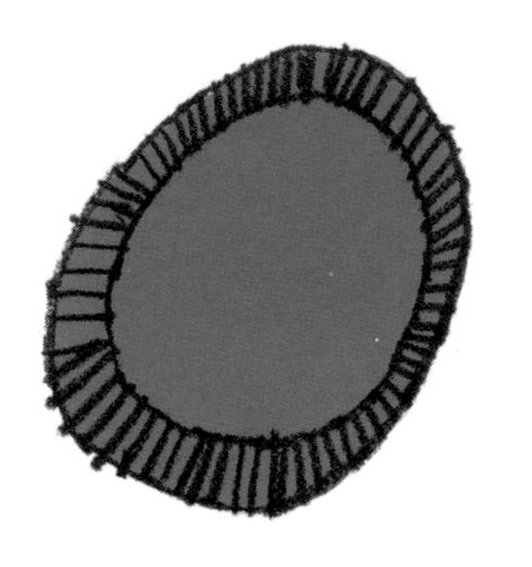

# The Further Adventures of SPIDER

West African Folktales
Retold by
JOYCE COOPER ARKHURST

Illustrated by
Caldecott Medal Winner
JERRY PINKNEY

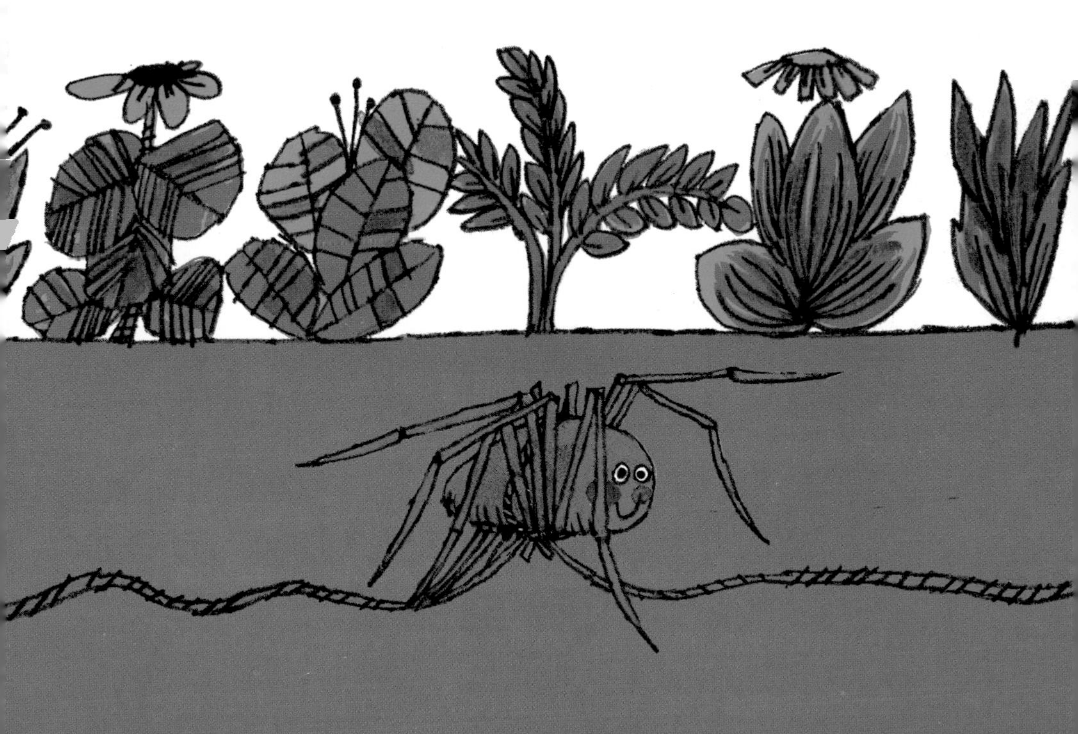

LB
LITTLE, BROWN AND COMPANY
New York Boston

*To all the friends in Liberia and Ghana who told me so many stories on so many moonlit nights.*

**This book is an abridged version of the story collection originally published as *The Adventures of Spider: West African Folktales.***



Little, Brown and Company

Hachette Book Group
237 Park Avenue, New York, NY 10017
Visit our website at www.lb-kids.com

Little, Brown and Company is a division of Hachette Book Group, Inc.
The Little, Brown name and logo are trademarks of Hachette Book Group, Inc.
The publisher is not responsible for websites (or their content) that are not owned by the publisher.

First Abridged Edition: November 2012

Originally published in *The Adventures of Spider: West African Folktales* in January 1964 by Little, Brown and Company

Library of Congress Cataloging-in-Publication Data
Arkhurst, Joyce Cooper.
The further adventures of Spider : West African folktales / retold by Joyce Cooper Arkhurst ; illustrated by Jerry Pinkney. — 1st abridged ed.
v. cm. — (Passport to reading level 4)
Summary: Presents abridged versions of three previously published tales of clever and crafty Spider, also called Anansi
Contents: How the world got wisdom — Why spiders live in dark corners — How Spider helped a fisherman.
ISBN 978-0-316-20345-6 (pbk.)
1. Tales—Africa, West. 2. Anansi (Legendary character)—Legends. [1. Folklore—Africa, West. 2. Anansi (Legendary character)—Legends. 3. Spiders—Folklore.] I. Pinkney, Jerry, ill. II. Title.
PZ8.1.A7Fur 2012
398.20966'0452544—dc23
2012005500

10 9 8 7 6 5 4 3 2 1

SC

Printed in China

# Contents

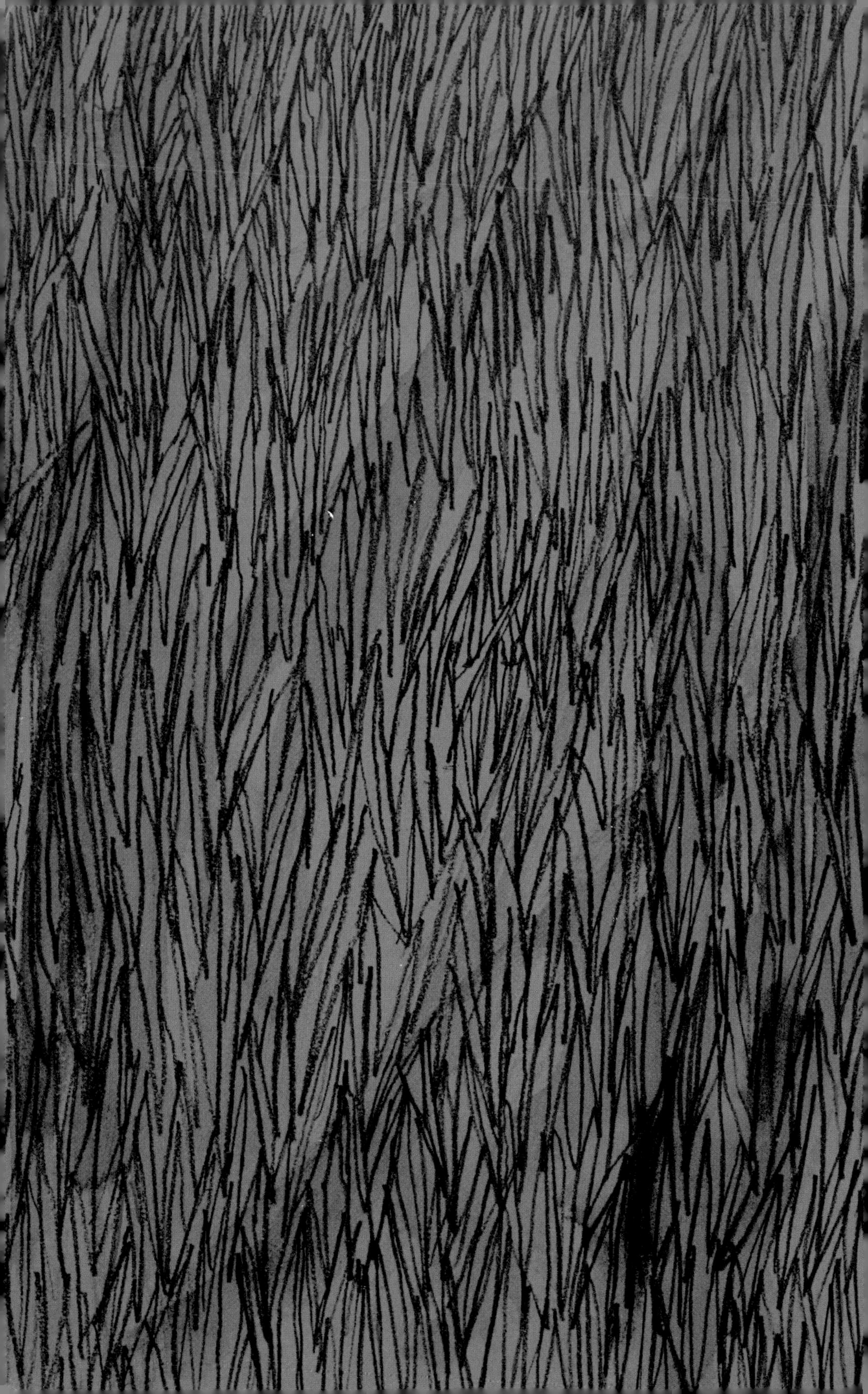

# Pronunciation Guide

| | |
|---|---|
| Akim | ah - KIM |
| Aso | ah - SOH |
| Kuma | koo - MAH |
| Nyame | nee - AH - mee |

## *Introduction*

IN WEST AFRICA people love to listen to stories. Sometimes at night, when the moon is high, everyone in the village comes out into the wide, clean place where people sit and talk.

Everyone sits in a circle. “Let us call the storyteller,” someone cries.

“Tell us a story about Spider,” cry the children.

Everyone knows about Spider. He is a favorite character in the stories of West Africa.

He is clever and mischievous. He loves to eat and he hates to work. He plays so many tricks that he gets into a lot of trouble. But when he is good, he is full of fun.

As the storyteller speaks, he strikes his stick upon the ground. “Once upon a time,” he says . . .

## *How the World Got Wisdom*

WHEN THE WORLD WAS very new, Nyame, the Sky God, gave all the wisdom in the world to Spider and told him to do whatever he wished with it. Of course, Spider wanted to keep it all for himself, and so he put it in a huge clay pot and covered it up tightly.

"One day I will become a king, for I will be the only wise man in the world," thought Spider.

He ran through the forest as fast as his eight legs would carry him, looking for a place to hide his pot of wisdom. He was in such a hurry that he didn't even answer when Tortoise and Hare asked him where he was going.

"I'll hide my wisdom in the top of the tallest tree in the world. No one will be able to climb it, because there are no branches near the ground."

But Spider was sure he could climb it himself. He had more legs than almost anybody else.

Spider tied his pot around his neck with a piece of strong rope and put his two top legs around the trunk of the tree as far as they would reach. He put the next two legs around the top of the pot, two more around the bottom of the pot, and the last two under the pot. Little by little, he began to go upward.

Spider was feeling very pleased, when suddenly he slipped. And he fell all the way back to the ground.

"Dear me," thought Spider. "I have eight legs. Surely I can climb this tree."

So he started again. But this time, his luck was no better than before. He fell right back down to the ground. Spider was getting angry. He decided to try once again. But no sooner did he get off the ground than BOOM! Down came Spider.

Now all this time, Kuma, Spider's eldest son, had been watching. "Father," said Kuma, "hang the pot behind you instead of in front of you."

When Spider heard this, he knew that Kuma had some wisdom, too, and that Spider could not have all the wisdom in the world to himself. This made him so angry that he threw the pot to the ground.

It broke into many pieces.

The good sense poured out in all directions. It made such a noise that people came from everywhere to see what it was. And when they saw the wisdom pouring out of the pot, they all reached down and took some of it. Even the animals got some. They spread it all over the world, and there was plenty to go around. Plenty for you and plenty for me.

## *Why Spiders Live in Dark Corners*

SPIDER LIVED IN a house made of banana leaves with his wife, Aso, and his two sons. Behind the banana-leaf house was a garden where they planted yams and corn and tomatoes, bananas, lemons, and oranges.

Every day Aso cooked rice and vegetables and meat and peppers into a big stew. It was delicious, and Spider ate until he could eat no more. You might have thought Spider would be satisfied, but of course he was not.

“What can I do?” Spider asked himself. “There are so many good things in my garden, and yet I can eat only half of them.”

Then he had an idea. He told his wife that he was not feeling very well and that very soon he would die.

Aso and her sons were sad, but Spider only said, “Since I am going to die soon, you must make a place to bury me. I want to put it here, just next to the spot where the tomatoes are growing.”

For Spider loved tomatoes best of all.

One day, very soon after, Spider pretended to get sick and die. Aso and her two sons shed

many tears and put Spider in his grave just beside the tomato patch. Spider stayed in the deep grave for several days because his family had a fine funeral, and many people came to mourn for him.

When it was finally over, Spider very quietly lifted the cover of the grave. The moon was so bright that he could see everything in the garden. He quickly picked several of the very best tomatoes. Then he pulled up some of the best yams. He cut off some green, juicy peppers and pulled up a few big onions. Then Spider crept into the chicken yard and plucked himself a nice fat chicken. When he had everything he wanted, Spider went back into his deep grave.

Now, it was not long after that Aso and her sons began to notice that something was happening to the garden. Every morning some of the best tomatoes and yams were missing. So Aso thought of a clever way to catch the thief. She brought a great pile of straw, and she built a man out of the straw. Then Aso covered him in soft, sticky beeswax. When she finished, she set him in the middle of the tomato patch.

That night, as soon as everyone was asleep, Spider crept out as usual. He was just about to pluck a big juicy tomato when he saw a man standing in the middle of his garden.

"Who are you?" Spider shouted. "What are you doing in my garden?" But instead of explaining himself, the man only looked at him.

"So! You won't talk?" asked Spider. "Then get out of my garden at once."

But still the man said nothing.

“I will teach you a lesson,” screamed Spider, and with that he hit the wax man as hard as he could with his right hand.

OOOF! His hand stuck fast in the beeswax. Spider pulled very hard, but he could not move it.

“So,” he yelled, “you are trying to be clever. I’ll show you.”

And he hit the wax man with his left fist. And that stuck, too.

“What is this?” cried Spider. “I’ll teach you a lesson.”

And with that he gave a mighty kick to the wax man. Now Spider was stuck hand and foot to the wax man.

“I’m stronger than you!” he shouted. And he gave the wax man a tight squeeze, and his stomach stuck fast to the wax man. Then he butted the wax man with his head as hard as he could. And, of course, his head stuck fast, too.

The next morning Aso and her two sons went into the garden to see whether they had caught the thief. At once they understood everything. The people in the village laughed at Spider and made up funny songs about him.

Spider was so ashamed of himself that he ran up into the darkest corner of the ceiling to hide. And he has lived there ever since.

## *How Spider Helped a Fisherman*

IN THE VILLAGE of Akim there was once a fisherman who worked very hard. Spider noticed how many big fish the fisherman brought to his house each evening. Spider was determined to find a way to get some for himself. So one day he went to see the fisherman and offered to help him.

But the fisherman knew all about Spider. He knew that Spider was greedy and lazy and always up to something. Yet when Spider asked if he could help him, the fisherman said, "Of course you can."

The people of Akim all laughed. "What a fool the fisherman is!" they said. "Spider will take all the fish, and the fisherman will do all the work."

But the fisherman only smiled.

On the first morning when Spider came to help, the fisherman said to Spider, "Now someone has to do the work and someone has to get tired, so we will take turns. One day you will be the one who gets tired, and I will do the work. The next day I will be the one who gets tired, and you will do the work. Today we will make traps to catch the fish. I will make the traps, and you will get tired."

"Me, get tired?" shouted Spider. "Indeed not. I will make the traps, and you will get tired!"

"Very well," said the fisherman, "if that is what pleases you." And he lay down on the ground as though he were very tired, while Spider made all the traps.

The following day the fisherman said to Spider, "My friend, today we must set the traps in the river. This time I will set the traps, and you will get tired for me."

"Never!" shouted Spider, and he set the traps in the water while the fisherman lay down on the bank. The fisherman moaned and groaned and rubbed his head and rolled about as if he were very tired.

"My oh my oh my!" he cried. "I'm *so* tired."

Well, on the third day the fisherman said to Spider, "Surely we must have a change today. I shall collect the fish from the traps, and you will be the one who gets tired."

"Do you think I am a fool?" Spider shouted. "You will get tired, and I will collect the fish."

"If you insist," answered the fisherman.

When the people of Akim walked past the river, they saw Spider busily gathering

fish and the fisherman lying on the bank looking very tired. But he kept his eyes fastened on Spider. So poor Spider did not get any fish at all.

On the final day, the fisherman said to Spider, “Today I will take the fish to market, and you will get tired.”

“Nonsense!” said Spider. “I will carry the fish to market, and you will get tired.”

And so Spider carried all the fish to market. When people came to buy, they paid the fisherman, because the fish belonged to him.

When all the fish were gone, the fisherman gave Spider four coins, one for each day he had worked. Spider saw that he had been tricked. He had very little of the money and none of the fish. At first he was angry, and then he simply burst out laughing at himself.

"Next time I will be the winner," he said. And he went merrily back to his little house among the banana leaves.

*One who plays tricks himself may be tricked if he is too greedy.*